Dear Reader,

This story is a █████████████████
Centennial continuity miniseries, the town of
Jasper Gulch, Montana, and its quirky citizens—
some a little sweeter than others and some
downright odd. My kind of folks!

Like all old towns, Jasper Gulch hides plenty of
secrets, and its legends are the stuff of dreams.
As each month unfolds featuring special events
in the Centennial Celebration, there will be a new
book by a different author to carry you through
from July 4 to Christmas and the new year. It's
my hope and prayer that you will enjoy visiting
Big Sky Country as much as I, Ruth Logan Herne,
Carolyne Aarsen, Brenda Minton, Jenna Mindel
and Arlene James have. We're looking forward to
seeing you at the centennial!

Blessings,

Valerie Hansen

Books by Valerie Hansen

VALERIE HANSEN

was thirty when she awoke to the presence of the Lord in her life and turned to Jesus. In the years that followed, she worked with young children, both in church and secular environments. She also raised a family of her own and played foster mother to a wide assortment of furred and feathered critters.

She loves to hike the wooded hills behind her house and reflect on the marvelous life she's been given. Not only is she privileged to reside among the loving, accepting folks in the breathtakingly beautiful Ozark Mountains of Arkansas, she also gets to share her personal faith by telling the stories of her heart in Love Inspired books.

Life doesn't get much better than that!

MONTANA REUNION
Valerie Hansen

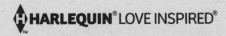

™ LOVE INSPIRED BOOKS

ISBN-13: 978-0-373-20811-1

MONTANA REUNION

Forget the former things; do not dwell on the past.
—*Isaiah* 43:18

**Big Sky Centennial:
A small town rich in history…and love.**

Her Montana Cowboy by Valerie Hansen, July 2014

His Montana Sweetheart by Ruth Logan Herne, August 2014

Her Montana Twins by Carolyne Aarsen, September 2014

His Montana Bride by Brenda Minton, October 2014

His Montana Homecoming by Jenna Mindel, November 2014

Her Montana Christmas by Arlene James, December 2014

To my Joe, who has always looked over my shoulder
while I write and always will.

Chapter One

"You don't say?"

"It's true! I saw her driving his pickup today with my own eyes."

"Probably because the roads are too slippery for a car."

"Or, she's taken up with him again. Imagine that!"

Annette Lakey wanted to laugh aloud. Instead, she kept working. She was happiest when the Cutting Edge Salon was busy. Customers like the one in her chair right now always kept her well entertained, so the time flew by.

Middle-aged Myrtle Kretsch, Mert for short, a waitress from Great Gulch Grub, was one of the most interesting storytellers, probably because her job at the café made her privy to plenty of gossip and wild tales.

Comb raised and scissors poised, Annette almost accidentally nicked her own finger when Mert grinned at their mutual reflections in the mirror and said, "I suppose you heard. Tony's back."

Meeting her own gaze, Annette realized her mouth had dropped open. She snapped it closed. "Tony Valdez?"

The older woman snickered like a teenager. "Yup. Rented the old Cosgrove house for a month, so they tell me, and moved in a few days ago. Guess he got fed up with city life and decided to give us another try."

"I can understand not liking the city," Annette said, hoping her nervousness wasn't noticeable. "Those of us who have half a brain stayed right here in Jasper Gulch where we belong."

"He's sure a good-lookin' rascal," the waitress remarked, continuing to study the slim young woman who was trimming her hair. "Filled out since he's been away, too. Not nearly as skinny as he was in high school."

"Neither am I," Annette told her with a nervous chuckle. "If I'd had all these curves when I was sixteen, maybe Tony wouldn't have stood me up for my junior prom and left town without even saying goodbye."

"I never knew that, honey. I'm so sorry. Didn't his family move away shortly after he got into more trouble with the law?"

"Yes. The kids who lit those fires in the old barns eventually confessed and cleared him, but by that time he and his folks were long gone—and I was stuck with a beautiful prom dress and nowhere to wear it."

"What a shame."

Shrugging and shaking off the gloomy memories, Annette managed to smile. "That's all water under the bridge. And speaking of bridges, how are the restoration plans for the one over Beaver Creek coming along?"

"Not so good. In a few months, after the centennial celebration kicks off, we should have a better idea of what we can and can't afford to repair." Mert rolled her eyes. "If Mayor Jackson Shaw wasn't such a…" She snickered. "Never mind."

"Hey, you don't have to tell me what our esteemed mayor is like. I grew up here, remember? If you look up the definition of *stubborn* in a dictionary you'll probably find his picture."

"You've got that right." Smiling, Mert paused to study the mirror again. "How do you think I'd look with a few of those crazy streaks of bright colors you've started putting in your hair?"

It took Annette a few moments to realize the older woman was teasing. "Hey, if you're game, I'll be glad to add some for you."

"Let's hold off, okay?" She glanced out the front window into the street. "Brrr. Looks like the storm's building. I thought winter was supposed to be all over by Easter."

"Me, too. Guess the good Lord decided we needed the rain."

"Rain? That looks more like sleet to me. I'm gonna freeze my fanny off getting back to work—if I don't slip and fall on it."

Annette sighed. "Which probably means I'll have a bunch of cancellations for tomorrow. Hopefully, the ice will melt off in a day or so."

The front door suddenly swung open, startling Annette and letting in gusts of freezing air. It was old Rusty Zidek, a well-known sight in the small Montana town. She was about to tell him to hurry and shut the door when she noticed that he wasn't alone.

At his feet, shivering and hunched over, was a small, mostly black, long-haired dog with wet, ice-encrusted fur. Annette's heart instantly melted. "Oh, you poor thing!"

Rusty gave her a grin that lifted the ends of his mustache and showed a gold tooth. "It is mighty cold out there."

"Not you," she countered with a grin. "Your dog. She looks frozen."

"That she is, ma'am," he replied. "Only thing is, she ain't mine. I just stumbled across her on my way to dinner." He eyed Annette's customer. "Figured if I took her with me to eat, Mert would have my hide. Since she's here, maybe I can get away with doin' it, after all."

"Not on your life," the waitress snapped back. "You want to get us shut down by the health department?"

"No sirree. I surely don't." His gaze shifted to Annette. "Guess she'll have to stay here with you."

"No way. I can't keep a dog in my shop, either."

"You could let her warm up in your apartment in the back," the old man suggested. "Just for a bit."

What could she say? The poor animal was suffering. "Oh, all right. Take her in back and see that she's comfortable. I don't have any dog food, though."

"That's no problem. I'll be glad to go to the store for you."

"I hate to put you out like that."

Rusty was already halfway through the shop, the dog at his heels. "It'll be my pleasure, Miss Annette. I knew you'd be a Good Samaritan."

"Am I that predictable?" she asked him.

He chuckled. "Yes'm. You have a heart of gold and everybody knows it."

"You're saying I'm a patsy."

The elderly man laughed hoarsely. "Yes, ma'am. You surely are."

Tony had never intended to return to Jasper Gulch. His memories of the rural community were not the best, nor was he eager to be faced with questions about his checkered past. The fact that a series of odd circumstances had lured him back there shortly after getting his degree was more than a surprise. It was a conundrum.

He'd initially resisted his former mentor's plea for help. Anybody in his position would have, he reasoned. But his conscience had eventually won out and he'd agreed. After all, the assignment was only for a few weeks. Since he was already familiar with Jasper Gulch, it made perfect sense for him to be the one to take over J.T. Paul's veterinary practice during the family emergency that had called the older man away.

Besides, as long as this foul weather lasted, few people would be venturing out for routine pet care. Chances were, he'd spend a lot of his time playing solitaire on the office computer or scanning help wanted ads for a permanent position somewhere else. Anywhere else.

Tony had few fond memories of the little Montana town. His parents had brought him to the place he'd viewed as the end of the earth when he was in high school, and his negative reaction had been to make everybody's life as miserable as possible. Only now, in retrospect, was he able to see that most of the problems he'd faced then had been due to his off-putting attitude and unwise associations with a rowdy crowd.

The office phone rang. The answering machine caught the call before Tony could reach the front desk. He snatched up the receiver just as a man's voice said, "Hello?"

"Sorry. I'm here. How can I help you?"

"Where's your receptionist?"

"I gave everybody else the day off because of the forecast. It's too dangerous to be out and about."

"This ain't Dr. Paul," the caller stated, sounding bothered.

"No, sir. This is Dr. Valdez. I'll be substituting for him for a short time. He's away on a family emergency."

"Well…"

"I assure you I'm fully qualified. Be glad to show you my diploma." *Which is still so new I haven't had time to frame it.*

"Valdez, Valdez. That name rings a bell."

Tony sought to change the subject. "Do you have a sick animal, sir?"

"Not exactly. I found a stray dog. She was near froze to death and I was gonna ask the doc to look her over."

"I'd be glad to do that. How soon can you be here?"

"Well, see, that's a problem. I just got her inside to warm up and I don't reckon I should make her go out again, 'specially since the heater in my old

Jeep is broke. I was hopin' maybe you could stop by here on your way home."

"How do you know it's on my way?"

"Even if it ain't, will you come? She don't look good at all."

Considering his vows to help animals and his promise to J.T. to take good care of his practice, Tony didn't see any way to refuse. In view of the foul weather, the caller was probably right about it being best to keep the already stressed dog as warm as possible.

"All right. Give me the address. I'll put a message on the answering machine that we closed early due to inclement weather and make a house call pretty soon."

"Dr. Paul picked a fine substitute." The caller cited a number on Main Street. "We'll be waitin'."

Mert was Annette's last appointment for the day, and she was already getting cancellations for the rest of the week. Rusty Zidek had made himself at home in one of her chairs and started leafing through a magazine before he'd nodded off.

She touched his shoulder. "Rusty? I hate to disturb your nap but I'm ready to close and you haven't brought me that dog food yet. Do you want me to go get it?"

He snapped to attention and yawned. "No, no. I

just needed a short nap. It plumb tuckered me out helpin' that poor dog out of the street."

"I looked in on her just now and she's sound asleep on a blanket in the corner of my kitchen," Annette said. "I'll put up my closed sign but leave the doors unlocked so you can let yourself in when you come back. Are you sure you don't want me to go instead?"

He settled his damp Stetson on his head. "Nope. It ain't far."

When she tried to hand him shopping money he backed off. "No need for that. I rescued her and I'll pay for her feed since you're givin' her a home."

"Whoa!" Hand raised, palm out, Annette stopped him. "I never said I was going to keep her. She's only here to get warm and rest a little."

"Whatever you say. I called the vet, too, and he promised to stop by. Keep an eye out for him, okay?"

"Sure. No problem. Be careful out there."

"Yes'm. Will do."

Scanning the nearly abandoned street as best she could through the stinging, blowing sleet, Annette watched Rusty pick his way cautiously to his Jeep. She might not know much about dogs, but she was well acquainted with Montana's weather. She'd be fortunate if any of her regulars showed up for their weekly appointments, let alone had walk-in business. Nobody in his or her right mind ventured out in a storm like this.

Except a lost dog, an old man with a tender heart and whoever was slowly working his way in her direction on foot. The figure was bent forward, leaning into the gale and clearly battling to keep his balance. He was clad in a jacket that looked more suited to the city and a ball cap he kept tugging lower on his forehead.

There was a piece of paper flapping in the man's hand. He wasn't even wearing gloves! Who in Jasper Gulch would be that foolish?

Because he had to use both hands to still the note, he let go of his cap. It took flight. He made a grab for it and missed. When he turned back to face her before ducking his head against the effects of the storm, she found it hard to catch her breath. That thick, dark hair. Those compelling eyes. He was older, of course, and condensation on the window dimmed his image, but there was no doubt in her mind.

The person headed for her shop was the former town bad boy who had ruined her prom, marred her good reputation and left her to listen to her mother's constant carping about it for months afterward. None other than Tony Valdez!

Chapter Two

Tony checked the numbers over the door, then reached for the handle, wishing his caller had bothered to tell him he was going to a business rather than a private residence.

His icy fingers smarted when he twisted the knob.

As the door swung open he quickly ducked inside and pushed it shut behind him before pausing to stomp his wet boots on the mat and shake water off his coat.

"Man, it's cold out there!"

The lack of a reply caused him to scowl and look around. His already labored breathing was not helped by the sight of the young woman who was staring back at him with wide, beautiful, hazel eyes.

He started to smile an instant before he realized he knew her. "Annette?"

"What are you doing here?"

"I got a call." Tony held up the scrap of paper. "A man said there was a sick dog at this address."

"What does that have to do with you?"

Ignoring her snappishness, Tony smiled and said, "I'm a veterinarian. Remember how I used to help out at the animal hospital when I was in high school? Well, that inspired me to eventually go to college and get my degree."

"That's mind-boggling."

"I know. I didn't show a lot of promise in my teens. Thankfully, I wised up."

Shaking her head, she studied him. "College. My mother will never believe it. She was always sure you'd end up in jail. Or worse."

"Yeah. Well, leaving Jasper Gulch for a fresh start turned out to be for the best."

"It didn't do much for me."

"I beg your pardon?"

"You deserted me. I stood up for you against half the town and my own parents and friends, yet you packed up and left without even saying goodbye."

"I wrote you a note."

Tony began to frown when she fisted her hands on her jeans-clad hips and declared, "You did not."

"I'm sure I did."

"Think again." Annette pointed to the door. "Now, go away."

"Only if there's no sick dog here. I did take an oath, you know."

Watching changing emotions cross her pretty face, he waited. Maturity had brought a blossoming beyond anything he'd ever imagined. She'd strengthened her independence, too, judging by the streaks of neon colors in her lush, dark hair and her bright red T-shirt with a sparkly logo that read, Beauticians Never Run With Scissors.

He could tell the moment Annette made her decision about him because her shoulders relaxed noticeably.

"All right." She gestured. "Go on. The dog's that way. Just don't get any funny ideas. My door's not locked and Rusty will be back any minute."

"Rusty Zidek? I thought I recognized the voice on the phone, but I never dreamed that old coot was still alive and kicking." Tony started toward the rear of the salon. "Must be something about living in the wilds of Montana that's good for his health."

Although Annette was following him, he thought he heard a tinge of humor in her voice when she said, "He's just too ornery to give in. When he passed ninety he said he was good for another ten years."

"He well may be, God willing." Tony scanned the cozy, combination living room and kitchenette they had entered. "You live here?"

"Yes. Since I had to rent the whole building anyway, I figured it made sense."

"That, it does. I was fortunate to find a short-term rental on the Cosgrove place. It's for sale and they figured it was better to have it occupied than sitting vacant."

"Maybe they were afraid of vandalism," Annette said cynically.

"Touché."

"Yeah, well, that wasn't very kind. Sorry."

"No need to apologize. I was a pretty wild kid and my so-called friends were worse. Some of the stuff we were blamed for was actually true, at least in part."

Tony heard her sigh as he turned his attention to his patient. Someone had placed a rumpled blanket in a corner and the damp, shivering animal was curled in the center. Kneeling and letting the dog sniff his fingers first, he asked, "What's her name?"

"I have no idea."

"Well, we should call her something."

"Okay, how about Stormy?" Annette said as Tony began a hands-on examination. "Is she going to be all right?"

"Once she warms up she should be. Do you have any chicken broth you could heat? Not too hot. Just take the chill off it for her."

"Of course. Sorry. I should have thought of that. I'm not used to having a pet."

Shifting position, Tony took a stethoscope from his pocket and used it to further assess the dog while he spoke soothingly. "Good girl, Stormy. That's right. Take it easy. It won't be long now."

As he straightened, he glanced over at Annette. She was standing in front of the stove, stirring the broth he'd asked her to warm.

"This is almost ready," she said, acting more relaxed now that she had a useful task.

"So is your furry friend," he said with a lopsided grin.

"I beg your pardon?"

"Stormy's not sick. She's about to have puppies."

If he hadn't wanted to keep the woman as calm as possible, he would have laughed out loud at her expression of astonishment. It was followed closely by disbelief.

"Are you sure?"

Tony nodded, his smile broadening. "Positive. You and old Rusty are about to become grandparents."

Annette's forehead furrowed. *"Oh, no!"*

"Oh, yes. Settle down. It's perfectly natural. You don't have to worry about her."

"Her? It's not the dog I'm worried about, it's my business. I can't have a bunch of puppies running wild in here. What will my customers think? Not to mention inspectors from the state board if they get wind of it."

"They'll think you're a kindhearted animal lover who did the right thing in an emergency." Tony watched his words sink in and mellow her expression.

"That's what this is? A real emergency? Can't you take her with you? You're the one with the diploma."

"And you're the one with the place she's chosen as her nesting area. See how she's piled up the blanket around her? That's no accident. She's happy here and getting ready for the big event."

"But, but…I don't know anything about birthing puppies." Scowling at him, she added, "What's so funny?"

"You are. What you just said sounds suspiciously like a line from the movie *Gone with the Wind.*"

It took Annette only a few heartbeats to come up with a snappy comeback. "My grammar is better."

He smiled. "Is that broth about ready?"

"I'm afraid it may be a little too hot," she admitted as she poured some of it into a soup bowl. "Think she'll mind if I don't serve her off my good china?"

Tony had to admire the way Annette had recovered from her snit so quickly. "That dish will be fine." He took it from her and tested it with one finger before offering it to the dog.

"Okay, what now? Do I have to boil water or something?"

His chuckle was heartfelt. The longer he was around this woman, the more he was reminded of why he'd had a crush on her as a teen. "I'll need clean towels, preferably ones you won't want to keep afterward, and a big pot of coffee."

"I understand needing the towels," Annette replied, "but what's the coffee for?"

It was all Tony could do to keep from laughing as he answered. "Me."

Rusty's entrance upon his return was so noisy that Stormy startled and barked. Then she circled her nest twice and lay back down, much to Annette's relief.

"I got some canned food, too," the old man announced as he stomped his boots on the mat before starting for Annette's apartment. "Any sign of the vet?"

Tony stood. "I'm here. Let me help you with that. What'd you do, buy out the store?"

"Pretty near. I figured it might be a while before Miss Annette had a chance to get more supplies."

"There are stockpiles of kibble at the animal

hospital, too. J.T. was always well prepared for anything."

"That, he was," Rusty said. "Where'd he go anyway? He never said a word to me about leavin'."

Annette had the answer. "According to Mert, his mother has been under the weather. I know we'd been praying for her at church on Wednesday nights. I assume he felt she needed him with her."

Tony was nodding. "That's what he told me when he phoned and asked me to come help out."

Annette's stomach tightened when she remembered Mert mentioning a month's rent and realized he was confirming his short-term plans. "Then you haven't actually moved back to Jasper Gulch?"

"Not to stay, no. J.T. promised to get back as soon as possible. Since I was available, I agreed to sub for him."

Rusty was frowning. "You're a real vet, right?"

"Sure am. I did a short stint for a place in Michigan right after graduation and they've agreed to keep a part-time job open for me as long as they can. If this were summer I'd probably have been permanently replaced already."

The mostly black dog whined, drawing everyone's attention.

Annette crouched to stroke the animal's damp fur and moved the empty dish out of the way. "It's okay, Stormy. We're right here." She looked up at the two men. "You are going to stay, aren't you? I really don't know anything about how to help her if I need to."

They both nodded after glancing soberly at each other. She suspected that Rusty was now more interested in defending her from Tony than in caring for the dog.

That was probably just as well, she told herself, particularly if the animal's labor went on for a long time. Seeing Tony again had already unsettled her emotions and left her on edge. The necessity of spending a lot of private time with him would not be good.

Not good at all.

Chapter Three

Tony was in a tight spot. His medical training required that he stay, while basic survival instincts urged him to flee. Clearly, Annette had wanted Rusty around for her sake, but in Tony's mind the protection factor worked both ways. He'd had enough experience with small-town gossip to anticipate plenty of problems. As soon as one of the local busybodies spotted him in this pretty woman's apartment, rumors would begin to fly and squelching them would be as hard as trying to stuff an irate cougar into a limp gunnysack.

He accepted a mug of steaming coffee from Annette, then settled himself on a kitchen chair and crossed an ankle over his opposite knee, noting that his jeans were almost dry. "Thanks. This could be a long night."

"I thought you said she was ready."

Rusty sipped from his own mug, wiped his mustache on his sleeve and answered for Tony. "Can't hurry Mother Nature, girl. These things take time."

"He's right," Tony added. "There's no point in giving her a shot to bring on harder contractions yet. It's best we let her do this with as little intervention as possible. If she gets too tired or shuts down, then I'll step in."

"How long do you think it will be?" Annette asked.

Tony shrugged. "Can't tell. Once she has the first pup the rest should follow pretty easily. The best thing we can all do is kick back and relax so we don't make her more nervous."

Watching Annette's expression change, he assumed she was coming to terms with their touchy situation. When she finally spoke, he was certain.

"In that case, I suppose I'd better plan supper for three." She smiled at the old man. "I know Rusty never got to the café this afternoon, and I assume you haven't eaten recently, either."

"It's not necessary to feed me," Tony said. "However, if you're fixing something, I might be able to eat a bite or two."

"I don't doubt it." Although there was no smile on Annette's face right then, he was positive he heard suppressed humor in her tone.

Tony checked his patient once more, then rose. "Is there something I can do to lend a hand?"

She arched an eyebrow. "Can you cook?"

"Well enough. I roomed with a couple of guys in college and we took turns. What do you have in the fridge to work with?" Instead of waiting for her to reply, he took several steps to the side, opened the refrigerator door and leaned to peer in.

"Not a lot," she said flatly.

Tony agreed. "You can say that again."

"Okay, not a—"

He interrupted and grinned at her. "Never mind. I get the picture." Inclining his head toward the other man, he asked, "How about takeout, Rusty? You game to go across the street and pick it up or do you want me to? My treat this time."

Although the geriatric cowboy got to his feet, apparently eager to oblige, Tony heard Annette's softly spoken "*This* time?"

"We may be done in a matter of hours," Tony explained to her. "Or, we might be ordering breakfast tomorrow morning. Can't tell yet."

Rusty was smoothing his mustache and smiling enough to show his gold tooth. "Guess he does know his stuff, after all. Suppose we get three blue plate specials tonight and extra pie for a snack later?"

"Sounds good to me," Tony said. He took out his wallet and handed several bills to the older man. "Will this cover it?"

"If it don't, I'll put the difference on my tab," Rusty assured him. "That order all right with you, Miss Annette?"

She rolled her eyes. "I wondered when the two of you were going to remember to ask *my* opinion."

Tony made a bowing gesture that he hoped would disarm her. Instead, it seemed to reinforce her already well-established contrariness.

She shooed Rusty toward the door. "Just go. If I don't like the special I can always eat a carton of yogurt and a piece of fruit for supper, the way I usually do."

The geriatric cowboy made eye contact with Tony and winked. "Good choice to order takeout, son. We'd likely have starved to death eating what Miss Annette has in her larder."

"I've been too busy to shop," she countered. "If I'd known to expect company I'd have planned ahead."

"Not company," Tony warned, as much to remind himself as his hostess. "This is strictly business. As soon as there's no more need for me, I'll be going."

When she said, "Good," he was surprised to note how much it bothered him.

As far as Annette was concerned, the idea of sharing a meal was a big mistake. Not only did the three of them gather around her kitchen table to eat, the men behaved as if they were lifelong buddies, leaving her feeling ill at ease in her own home.

"I thought I recognized your voice on the phone," Tony told Rusty.

"Well, it has been a coon's age since you high-tailed it out of here."

"Nearly ten years," Tony replied.

Annette kept her eyes on the take-out container in front of her, poking a slab of lukewarm pot roast and watching the gravy pool.

Rusty kept talking, bringing up ancient history that she would just as soon have left buried. "I heard tell you were cleared of that barn burning back then. That true?"

"Yep." Tony nodded. "I wasn't a real delinquent, although I may have done some damage with spray paint and gone along when my friends pulled a few other pranks."

"Boys will be boys," Rusty remarked. "We have a whole new generation of rascals now. I don't suppose you remember Pete Daniels. He'd have been much younger back in the day, when you were getting into trouble."

"Nope. At least I never caused any real destruction." Tony began to grin. "Not that my folks believed my alibis. They thought they were rescuing me when they packed up and moved." He heaved a noisy sigh. "In a way, I suppose they were, since it also led me to eventually get right with God."

It startled Annette to hear him confess his faith, and she was even more stunned when he swung his attention back to her and added, "I never meant to hurt you."

"That was a long time ago," she countered softly. "Forget it."

"You haven't forgotten."

"When you're right, you're right. Seeing you again did remind me of a lot of things best forgotten."

She watched as he nodded, took a bite of food and chewed slowly.

When he finally looked at her, she was surprised to note how subdued his demeanor had become. "There was a lot going on in my life back then, Annette. My parents were panicking about my future and positive they'd raised a budding criminal, my teachers were threatening to keep me from graduating because my grades had slipped so low and the school had given notice I might be expelled over my arrest. All in all, I think I did well to remember anything."

"You could have at least phoned to tell me you were leaving." It distressed her to detect a hint of unintended pathos in her voice. This was all supposed to have been put behind her, so why did it still hurt so much to remember?

"By that time I was already persona non grata all over town, if you'll recall. Your parents hadn't liked me from the beginning, and after I came under suspicion of setting that fire, I knew they'd be furious if I tried to talk to you."

"You could have called my cell."

"I know. And you'd have had to lie if they'd asked you about me." To his credit, Tony looked ashamed. "So I took the coward's way out and wrote you a note."

Jaw set, Annette shook her head. She was not about to let him get away with such a transparent fib. After all, she was no longer the impressionable teen he'd once fooled. "Nice try, Valdez. There was no note."

"Wait a minute. What about my letters? I sent them without a return address on the envelope so nobody would suspect who they were from. Are you saying you didn't get those, either?"

"Nope." She rolled her eyes and arched her eyebrows. "You may as well stop wasting your time making lame excuses. We both went on with our lives after a silly, teenage crush and that's that. What amazes me now is that you came back at all."

"I won't be here for long."

Good thing, she thought wryly before smiling and saying, "I'll be sure to keep that in mind."

The sun had long ago set. Rusty was nodding off in the only comfortable chair in the apartment while Tony busied himself rechecking Stormy. Her abdomen was tightening on a regular basis and she'd begun to pant.

Soft footsteps behind him drew his attention and he smiled up at Annette.

"Is she all right? Can I get her some more broth? She's acting awfully thirsty."

"The panting is normal. I doubt she'll drink or eat anything more until she's done."

"Oh."

"Is there any hot coffee left?" Tony asked.

"A little. I'll make more if we need it."

Tony let himself smile as he glanced toward the old man. "Looks as though caffeine doesn't keep Rusty up at night."

"Nothing stops him from napping when he's tired." She returned with the pot and refilled Tony's mug before topping off her own and adding cream and sugar.

"Must be how he's lasted so long. He listens to his body's natural rhythms. I've often thought we'd all be healthier if we slept when we were tired and ate when we were hungry instead of letting our lives be dictated by clocks and schedules."

Annette's soft laugh sent tingles up Tony's spine before she said, "I imagine my customers would object if I stopped in the middle of a perm and rested. They'd end up looking like one of Julie's sheep."

"Julie? That name sounds familiar."

"It should. Julie Shaw's dad is the mayor. You probably knew her older siblings. Cord is the eldest, then there's Austin, Adam and Faith."

"I do recall some of the Shaws. What's with the sheep business?"

"Julie raises them for wool, mostly. She's got quite a successful operation, particularly on the internet."

"Interesting." His focus shifted to the blanket as the dog circled twice, then settled again before bending around and beginning to pay more attention to her other end. "Hold on. Here we go."

He picked up one of the clean white towels and was soon helping dry a squirming, whining puppy. The expression of wonderment on Annette's face brought him almost as much joy as holding the new life in his hands.

"It's beautiful!" There were unshed tears in her eyes. "I've never seen anything like this before."

"Then you've missed a lot," Tony told her. "I'm going to put this baby back down so Stormy doesn't get worried. If she isn't careful enough, I may have to hand you one or two to hold and keep warm while she has the rest."

"I'd love to hold one." She reached out.

"Not yet. It's always best to let animals do things their way if possible. You'll have plenty of time to play with them later."

"Later? How much later?"

The way her jaw dropped when he said, "They'll be weaned and on their way to new homes in about eight weeks," almost made him laugh out loud.

Chapter Four

"It was a dark and stormy night," Annette commented. Looking through the front window of her shop, she could see wet sidewalks by the glow of the antique street lamps. The rain was slacking off, but since the outside temperatures were still low there was no question of transporting Stormy, or her new babies, to any other location. Not yet anyway.

She returned to the blanket and newly arrived litter. "Is that all there are? Do you think she's done?"

Kneeling, Tony nodded and rocked back on his heels. "Yes. I palpated her. There were only these four pups."

"Why does one look so different from the others?"

"You mean the spotted gray-and-white and

cinnamon-colored one? She either had a different daddy than the others or Stormy carries a recessive gene for lighter coat color. Could be both. It's impossible to tell unless you want to spring for a DNA test, and even then you wouldn't know much more than the basic breeds in their background."

"Hmm. Well, it's awfully early to be certain, but that little one looks like the spitting image of Julie's dog, Cowboy Dan. He's an Australian shepherd."

"Which would explain why her tail is naturally bobbed," Tony added.

"It *is?*" Annette wasn't too weary to appreciate the significance of the very short tail. "Wait till I tell Julie. She'll be so excited!"

"Unless she thinks you're cooking up a paternity suit," Tony gibed. "Maybe it would be best to just invite her to see the litter and let her come to her own conclusions."

"Right. I will."

Now that the excitement was over, Annette began to gather up the soiled terry cloth. "Ick. I see why you warned me to bring you old towels."

"Sorry. You won't be able to bleach those enough to use them in your shop again, but they will make good scrubbing cloths."

She paused and inclined her head to one side to give him a quizzical look. "Scrubbing? Scrubbing what?"

"Whatever." Tony's glance darted back to the occupants of the blanket.

"Oh, no. I am *not* keeping those dogs."

"Okay. Fine with me. For the present, however, you and I both know they're safer and happier right where they are. Poor Stormy's had a rough night."

"And we haven't?"

"You and I may have. Rusty slept through the best parts."

She huffed. "All right. They can stay for a little while. But as soon as she's rested enough, they all have to leave."

Although Tony was nodding sagely, she strongly suspected that he was not in total agreement. He knew, as did Rusty, that she was too tenderhearted to boot the poor dog and her babies out into the cold. Annette didn't deny that she had already formed an attachment to the brood. After all, she'd seen them born and heard their first little mews, as if they were baby kittens instead of robust pups.

They were sleeping now, snuggled next to their mother after having nursed, while Stormy took a well-deserved snooze. Gazing down at them, Annette could not help feeling as if she was already a part of their lives.

"Where will you be taking them?" she asked.

"I suppose there might be room at the dog pound over in Ennis."

"No! You can't send them there."

"Then what do you suggest?" Judging by Tony's lazy smile and nonchalant pose, thumbs hooked in his jeans pockets, she had just committed herself. Unfortunately, he was right about the lack of good options, particularly in such forbidding weather. Any ranchers who might have adopted Stormy and the pups would be too busy caring for livestock right now to bother with a stray dog. Even Julie Shaw, who was a real altruist in regard to helpless animals, would be up to her neck in newborn lambs and stressed-out ewes.

"Okay, here's what we'll do. I'll take a picture of Stormy tomorrow and make up flyers to post around town. She's so gentle and sweet, I know somebody must be missing her. And until her owner claims her, she can stay with me, providing she behaves."

"As long as you keep her fed and exercised, she should do a good job of keeping you from being lonesome," Tony said.

"Who said I was lonesome, huh? I like my own company just fine." She wanted to ask what made him think she wasn't content to be by herself but chose to quit while she was ostensibly ahead.

"Okay. Whatever. If we don't hear something in a day or so, I'll come back and build you a puppy box."

"A what?"

"A big, open, wooden box with sides that are

low enough for Stormy to come and go on her own but will keep the pups from following her."

"Following her where?"

Annette made a wry face when Tony began to chuckle and said, "Outside. Unless you plan to teach her to use your bathroom, I suggest she be let out regularly."

"Oh, that. I told you I wasn't used to having pets, particularly not ones kept in the house. My mother never wanted to put up with the mess." She looked toward the blanket and her five new room-mates. "I can certainly see her point."

"All you need is a regular schedule," Tony told her. "Once Stormy has you properly trained, there won't be nearly as many problems."

"You mean, once I have *her* trained, don't you?"

Casting a lopsided smile at the dogs, then raising it to Annette, Tony shook his head. "Nope. You're new at this. Stormy is an old pro. I'll be real surprised if you're the one who makes her adjust to your lifestyle instead of the other way around."

Raising her chin and stiffening her spine, Annette stood firm. "I will not keep her one more second if she causes me too much grief. Got that?"

By this time Tony's grin had broadened and his dark eyes sparkled with mirth. "Oh, yeah. I understand perfectly. The question is, does Stormy?"

* * *

Tony knew he should have gone back to the Cosgrove house or stopped by the animal hospital to see if the techs had come back to work now that the storm was over. Anything but linger at Annette's. Instead, he crossed the street, ducked into Great Gulch Grub and ordered three take-out breakfasts.

Rusty met him at the door to the Cutting Edge when he returned. "One of those for me?"

"Sure is. I figured we could all use some ham and eggs." Tony smiled. "If Annette wants yogurt instead, Stormy can enjoy her meal."

The old man had donned his heavy coat and battered Stetson. "Much obliged, but I'll have to take a rain check. Can't miss my regular date with Mert. She'd pitch a fit if I wasn't there to rankle her of a morning."

"But…"

"Not to worry," Rusty told him. "I heard Miz Annette phoning Miz Julie, so it'll be the two of them against one, if you get my drift. Nobody's gonna think you're gettin' outta line."

"I suppose you're right to worry about Annette's reputation. No matter how much good I do in Jasper Gulch, I'll always be remembered as the kid who got into trouble, way back when."

The gold tooth flashed in a beam from the rising sun. "Leastwise you wasn't guilty."

"You're right. I wasn't guilty of anything except making poor choices of friends. Annette was one of the few people who gave me the benefit of the doubt. I just didn't appreciate it enough back then."

Rusty's grin broadened. "Maybe the good Lord is givin' you another chance."

That notion had occurred to Tony more than once in the past few hours, but he wasn't anywhere near ready to accept it. "Like I told you, I'm not here to stay. This is just a temporary assignment I agreed to in order to pay back an old friend."

Frowning, Rusty leaned closer to continue. "Just see that you treat *all* your old friends right this time, son. When the time comes for you to skedaddle, be sure you bid everybody a proper goodbye."

"I will. I promise."

The old man's characteristic smile reappeared. "In that case, what're we standin' here for? You'd best tote that food inside before it gets cold."

"Thanks for sticking around last night. I know Annette appreciated it." He paused, noticing the satisfied expression on Rusty's lined face. "Are you sure you didn't know I was in town when you phoned J.T.'s office?"

"'Course I knew. Everybody did."

"Even Annette?"

"Maybe. Good thing her shop was still open when that storm hit, wasn't it? Otherwise I might have had to leave the poor dog outside. It pains me to see any animal suffer like that."

"You knew all along that she was about to have pups, didn't you?"

"Doesn't matter either way. Stormy needed a home and Annette needed company. Far as I know, she's never had a real live pet, not even when she was little." His eyes twinkled and his ruddy complexion warmed. "In case you haven't noticed, she's all grown up now."

Tony rolled his eyes and nodded. "It just doesn't matter. I'd rather take up residence in the Amazon jungle than stay in Jasper Gulch."

"Have it your way," Rusty told him sagely before touching the front brim of his hat politely and passing him on his way across Main to the café.

"I *am* doing this my way," Tony muttered to himself. The only thing that bothered him about that statement was the possibility that he had somehow failed to notice God in the details.

Chapter Five

Annette had considered thanking Tony for the early-morning meal while not actually eating it, but by the time he'd opened the take-out containers and handed her a fork, the delicious aroma of the food had overcome her reticence.

Then, when Julie arrived to view the pups she was able to relax more. "They're right over here. Look!"

Her friend passed Tony without giving him more than a cursory glance. "Oh, I see what you mean. The little gray one is adorable." Julie gently lifted it. "And she has a short tail, too. She certainly does look like my Dan."

"I told you so," Annette said. "Will you stay for breakfast? We have plenty." Gesturing at the table, she added, "Remember Tony Valdez? He's a vet now."

"Really? I thought those rumors were crazy."

Tony grinned. "Nope. I have proof back at the animal hospital if you want to see it."

"Maybe later, if I decide to use you for my sheep." Julie seated herself between him and Annette. "How long is Dr. Paul going to be away?"

"Don't know for sure. Probably a month or so." Tony got up and added an empty mug to the ones already on the table. "Coffee, Ms. Shaw?"

"Yes, thanks, and you may as well call me Julie. I'm sure you remember me as a little kid."

"You did trail after Adam and Austin a lot," Tony replied.

"True. Cord usually managed to ignore me, but my other brothers were happiest when they were teasing or ditching me. Being the youngest is the pits."

"Which reminds me," Annette said, "do you have any idea how that little gray puppy ended up looking enough like Cowboy Dan to be his twin?"

"A lot would depend on where Stormy came from," Julie said. "What did Rusty tell you about her?"

"Very little. He said he found her wandering the streets during the storm, but she seemed awfully obedient when he led her through the shop."

"Could he have been setting you up?"

"For what? If he wanted me to adopt a dog, all he had to do was ask me."

"Would you have taken her in if it hadn't been an emergency?" Julie asked wisely.

Blinking rapidly, Annette studied her old friend, then shifted her attention to Tony with a scowl. "Did you have anything to do with all this?"

He leaned back, hands raised, palms facing out. "No way. I am totally innocent, ladies. I didn't even know you had opened a beauty shop when I arrived. Remember?"

"That's true. You did look genuinely surprised. I certainly was."

He arched an eyebrow. "Were you? Julie knew. I'd assumed the local grapevine would have informed you, too."

"That you were in town, yes. That you were a practicing veterinarian, no." She gave him a lopsided smile. "Even if somebody had told me that, I wouldn't have believed it."

"Oh, I don't know," Julie said. "Now that I think back, he did help out at the animal hospital when we were younger. I remember because I was so involved in 4-H and FFA."

"That's right." He took a sip from his coffee mug. "Annette tells me you've turned your Future Farmers of America project into a going wool business. Good for you."

"Thanks. I have been blessed. Dad even lets me pasture my flock on Shaw land, which is a big concession from a cattleman like him. I keep expecting the other shoe to drop, but so far I've managed to keep him happy, particularly by staying out of the argument about whether or not to repair the Beaver Creek bridge and encourage tourist traffic."

Tony leaned farther back in his chair and made a face as if he'd suddenly remembered something distasteful. "Some things never change, do they? Small-town politics is alive and well in good old Jasper Gulch."

"It's a lot more than that," Annette chimed in. "We've been planning a big centennial celebration that's going to last from this coming July to the end of the year. Mayor Shaw is on board with most of it, like the opening parade on the Fourth of July and a big rodeo that month. It's how we should spend the revenue we expect to generate that's pitted some of the committees against each other."

"All the more reason for me to be glad I'm only going to be here for a short time," Tony said flatly. "If there's a rodeo coming, that's likely to mean a lot more large-animal work. I'm not eager to get stomped or kicked by livestock that weighs a ton. Literally."

"J.T. never seemed to mind," Julie said. "I think he prefers working outside to being stuck in his office."

"Different strokes for different folks," Tony replied. "I'm trained for all of it, but I like my patients small and cute and fluffy."

"Like Stormy's pups," Annette said with a soft sigh. "I can't believe how adorable they are. When they sleep they twitch and move their little paws as if they're dreaming."

"That's a sign of good health," Tony told her. "A lethargic newborn can indicate a problem."

Annette set aside the remainder of her breakfast and studied him as she asked, "What else do I need to know? There must be a lot to learn. How will I be sure they're doing okay?"

When Tony said, "I suppose I could drop by a few times to check on them," she nearly sighed with relief. If his suggestion had not also meant that her strained nerves would also keep tingling due to his presence, she would have felt a lot better about the offer. "I'll pay you, of course," Annette promised. "I'm not asking for charity."

"I didn't think you were. And while we're on that subject, since Rusty Zidek was the one who called me in the first place, I plan to send him the bill for last night."

"Oh, dear." She clasped her hands together tightly. "Will it be very expensive?"

Smiling, Tony replied, "No. The house call was his idea, but staying for hours was mine, so I won't bill according to that."

"Oh, good!"

Julie brightened. "Hey, if you're offering bargain rates, you can come to my place and help me dock tails this afternoon."

The look of distress that flashed over Tony for an instant almost made Annette chuckle. She reached out and laid a hand lightly on his forearm. "Don't worry, Doc. She's just teasing. She and the boys handle that minor surgery fine by themselves."

Expecting him to mirror her good humor, Annette noticed him focusing on her hand—and his arm—instead. She withdrew as if she'd just touched a hot stove. "Sorry."

"No problem," he said flatly as he pushed his chair back and got to his feet. "I need to get to work and check my messages, then take care of whatever patients I may have today. How late do you keep the shop open?"

"Why?"

"Because I want to try to be back here before you close for the day. There's no sense starting rumors if we can avoid it."

"Are you scared of me?" She'd meant the question to be humorous, but when Tony looked straight into her eyes and said, "Not of you, of myself," Annette felt her heart begin to hammer.

However, as soon as he added, "I don't intend to get personally involved here," she understood his motivation. It wasn't that he feared his attraction to her would overwhelm his moral code. He wasn't protecting *her*. He was insulating himself against the possibility that there might still be a lingering spark of fondness for her in his heart.

In a way, that notion buoyed her spirits. In another way, his firm resolve was terribly disappointing.

Tony rechecked Stormy, then asked for something to use as a makeshift leash and was given a long, red ribbon. He led the weary dog out the rear door, ostensibly to spare Annette the trouble.

Truthfully, he was eager to distance himself from her, particularly since their casual conversation had taken a giant leap into the touchy area of personal feelings. He hadn't meant to reveal so much, nor had he expected such a strong reaction when she had touched his arm. This was only his second working day in Jasper Gulch and already he'd encountered trouble.

The worst aspect was his inability to do anything about it. His job demanded that he be diligent no matter what counterargument his emotions came up with. He was a vet first and a man second. His training insisted that he offer the best care possible, and if that meant returning to the beauty shop to check Stormy and her pups, then so be it.

Turning up the collar of his jacket, Tony stood with his back to the wind and watched the dog sniffing the ground. She'd recovered well, so far, and it looked as if she wouldn't need any additional injections. The pups seemed healthy, too.

"So, I won't have to come back often," he argued, realizing that a daredevil part of his psyche was at war with the more stoic side. He truly did not have to return to Annette's shop. He could simply insist that she or Rusty bring the puppies to the animal hospital for their exams and first puppy shots, instead.

As Stormy led him back to the door they'd exited from, Tony realized he was going to do nothing of the kind. He was going to continue to make house calls, to see Annette, to risk his heart, because, in spite of everything in their shared past, he still cared for her.

"So, what's with the overnighter?" Julie asked Annette while Tony was walking the dog. "I can't believe you let him stay."

"It was strictly business. Besides, Rusty was here, too. He's the one who got me into this mess."

Chuckling, Julie scanned the nest of pups. "Looks like it's a good thing you have a big washing machine. Those little guys and their mama are going to give it a workout."

"That's what I'm afraid of."

"You're going to need a way to keep them in one place soon. I could bring you one of the portable kennels I use for weak or sick lambs, but I think you'd be better off with a box that Stormy can leave at will."

"That's what Tony said."

"He did, did he? What else did he say?"

"That he'd build something for me out of wood if I wanted him to." She made a face that showed bewilderment. "What should I do?"

"That depends," her old friend replied. "What do you want to do?"

Annette rolled her eyes. "Beats me. I thought I was content to stay single and concentrate on running my business—until Tony showed up again. Right now, I think I'm more confused about him than I was at sixteen."

"Uh-oh. That's not good."

"You're telling me! He's better looking and settled now, but he keeps insisting he's not going to stick around. I love Jasper Gulch. My whole life is here. I'd be an idiot to let myself fall for him again."

"True." Julie was nodding sagely. "But I saw the way you two looked at each other this morning during breakfast. If you ask me—and you did—I think it's less a matter of falling in love again than it is of acknowledging that you've never fallen out of love in the first place."

"That's impossible. We were just kids."

"I know." Pausing to gather their trash while helping clear the table, Julie finally went on, "I guess my question should be, 'What did you think when he walked in here?' Were you happy or angry or what?"

"Or what," Annette quipped. "I was mostly stunned."

"And then what happened?"

"I don't remember, exactly. I think I told him to go away before I found out he was a vet and Rusty had called him. I'd forgotten that J.T. was gone."

"Would it have mattered if you'd known Tony was taking his place? You still needed medical help."

"True." She sighed as she rinsed her hands at the kitchen sink. "I feel like Alice right after she fell down the rabbit hole. Everything is so *wrong*."

Julie grinned and waggled her eyebrows. "Oh, yeah? Are you sure of that?"

Chapter Six

Rather than ask for permission to revisit later in the week and chance being refused, Tony decided to simply show up at Annette's during his lunch break a few days later. He gathered several two-by-twelve boards, cut them to length and used J.T.'s truck to haul them to the rear of the beauty shop so he could construct the puppy box on-site.

The wind was still blowing enough to cause a chill, but at least the ice on the streets had disappeared.

The only reply he got to his knock at the back door was the sound of a dog's nails scratching on the inside, so he eased open the door and called, "Anybody home?"

"Come on in," echoed from the front of the salon.

Tony knew it was Annette issuing the invitation. What puzzled him was that she wouldn't bother to check who was there. Was it possible she'd recognized his voice easily, too?

Sidling past the excited mama dog, he headed down the hallway connecting the living quarters to the business section of the old brick building.

"It's me," Tony announced with a smile and a wave to Annette and her customers. "Afternoon, ladies."

One was seated in a swivel chair, her head nearly covered in separate, layered pieces of folded foil, while another customer peered out from under a hair dryer.

His smile broadened and settled on Annette. "You building a robot there or trying to get better radio reception?"

"Kind of looks like that, doesn't it? This is to keep the color from bleeding into the rest of her hair."

"If you say so." Tony gestured toward the apartment. "I brought the wood to build you the box like I promised. Mind if I go ahead with it?"

"I guess not. While you're back there, would you please take Stormy for a short walk? I didn't have much time this morning and she's probably waiting to go out again."

"Sure. No problem. I just didn't want you to panic if you heard me banging around."

"I can join you as soon as I give Mamie her comb-out."

Bending at the waist, Tony peered at the scowling face beneath the hair dryer. "Ms. Fidler? Are you still running the inn? I called and tried to book a room there before I rented a house, but you were full."

"It's been a good year," the older woman said flatly.

Apparently sensing her client's grouchiness, Annette took over the conversation. "And it promises to do nothing but get better from now 'til the end of December."

Tony was momentarily puzzled. "It does?"

"Yes, because of the centennial celebration I told you about. Remember? You said you hoped J.T. got back before the rodeo started."

"I still do hope so." Tony waved to all the women as he said, "Nice to see you ladies again. I'll get out of your hair now."

When Annette started to grin, he realized he'd inadvertently made a joke, so he followed it up. "The only grooming I intend to do is on your new dog."

"I told you, I don't own a dog," Annette was quick to reply. "I'm only letting her stay here because I can't bear the thought of her ending up in an animal shelter."

"Did you make those flyers you mentioned?"

"I haven't had time yet. I will."

Tony knew a lame alibi when he heard one. Annette hadn't gotten around to posting lost-and-found flyers because she was enjoying Stormy's company and was in no hurry to see her reclaimed.

That was just as well. The dog was obviously content to stay at the beauty shop, and as long as Rusty continued to insist he didn't know the animal's origin, she'd be safe and warm right where she was.

Plus, it would be good for Annette to have a constant companion, even if she did deny being lonely. He'd spent plenty of solitary time of late and didn't particularly enjoy being totally by himself. Maybe, if he was still in town when the pups were weaned and given away, he'd volunteer to take Stormy or one of her babies with him.

Although the part-time position he'd held when J.T. had asked for his help was a step in the right direction, it was sadly insufficient for the future. Nevertheless, he'd been glad to get it. As a new graduate he'd needed to enhance his résumé. This stint in Montana would help do that, too.

As he walked down the hall, he muttered to himself, "And when I leave, I can ask for references."

Stormy greeted him, wiggling all over, and raced to the door, where she ran in tight circles.

"I see you *are* ready for another walk," Tony

said gently. "Okay. First I'll give your babies a quick look and then we'll go explore."

All four pups were piled together on a freshly laundered blanket and surrounded neatly by a ridge of bath towels. Not only were they content, their little stomachs were full.

Tony patted the proud mama dog on the head and commended her for doing a good job while she gave her brood her own cursory inspection.

The wrinkled, slightly frayed length of red ribbon was looped over the knob on the back door, leading him to conclude that Annette was still using it as a leash.

"I'll have to bring you a proper collar and lead," Tony told Stormy. "Come on, girl. Let's go take a tour of Jasper Gulch and see what kind of mischief we can get into."

Judging by her eagerness and panting, joyful expression, she would have given a loud "Hooray!" if she'd been able to speak.

By the time Annette was free to check her apartment, the rectangular puppy playpen was nearly complete.

"I didn't hear any hammering. I thought maybe you'd gone."

"I'm using screws so we can take this apart more easily when you're done with it. No sense wasting good lumber."

She stood back and eyed the box. "It's bigger than I thought it would be."

"They'll grow into it. Besides, Stormy needs room to sleep without being pestered by these hungry little guys."

"I wondered about that," Annette said. "When I looked them over this morning, their tummies were really bulging. Are they supposed to eat so much?"

"Unlike people, most animals will stop when they get full. The only ones who obsess about food are those who may have been deprived in the past."

"Okay, you're the doctor." She sank into a kitchen chair and stroked Stormy's fur while Tony continued to use a power drill to set the final screws. "I still can't believe it. How in the world did you go from town bad boy to a college graduate?"

"I admit I made a few detours. That's why it took me so long. The important thing is, I made it."

"Hmm. I always thought you had more potential than you showed." She smiled at the sweet memories. "That's why I stood by you, even after most of the town decided you were guilty of vandalism and even arson."

"I'd hoped you weren't thinking the worst of me. I was never positive."

"You should have been. I told you often enough."

Tony sat back on his heels and looked at her.

She imagined she could see his internal struggle and likened it to her own. Were they really so far apart emotionally? Or was she visualizing a connection where there was none, simply because her heart kept insisting they could recapture the tender feelings they'd once shared?

Tony was shaking his head slowly, contemplatively. "If you did tell me, it never registered. I guess I was too full of myself and too concerned with maintaining a rough, tough reputation to listen." His dark eyes made contact with Annette's. "I never meant to hurt you, or to stand you up the way you claim. I've been racking my brains and I *know* I left you a note."

"Nope."

"Like I told you, I wrote letters, too." He stood to look down at her, his expression somber. "I may have been an idiot back then, but I didn't lie to you. And I didn't ditch you without saying goodbye."

"It doesn't matter anymore."

"I think it does. Do your parents still live around here?"

"They moved away after Dad retired. Why?"

Tony handed her his cell phone. "Call your mother and ask her about my note and my letters."

"Are you joking?"

"Dead serious."

She pressed her lips into a thin line. "Mom

probably won't even remember I had a crush on you back then."

"I think she will," Tony said with conviction. "Why else would she keep my letters from you?"

Staring at him, Annette began to scowl. "Are you calling my mother a liar?"

All he did was arch one dark eyebrow and give her a quizzical look.

"I don't believe this. I thought you'd become a sensible adult, but you're still playing childish games with people's feelings. My parents raised me to tell the truth and be an upright citizen, just like they are. For you to even suggest otherwise is a slap in the face to the mom and dad I love and respect."

"So, you aren't going to ask her?"

"Of course not. And I'm not going to tell her about your unfair insinuations, either. You're being totally ridiculous. If I didn't get your letters and you really did write to me, they probably just got lost in the mail."

"*All* of them? Okay, whatever you say, Annette." Tony gathered up his tools and the few screws he'd had left over. "I'm *done* here."

The possibility that his statement harbored a double meaning was not lost on her. The finality of his words left little doubt that he was finished trying to explain himself, as well as done constructing the box.

"Stormy and her babies thank you," Annette said. Considering the animosity in Tony's expression when he glanced at her, he knew exactly what she'd meant by excluding herself. It was going to be a cold day in August before she forgave him for slandering her innocent mother.

As soon as Tony slammed out the back door, however, she began to feel a deep sense of loss. There was something about having him around that cheered her. Normally it did, anyway. Now that he was gone and clearly upset, she wanted to follow him, to soothe his hurting heart, to bring back his warm, loving smile.

She would not, of course. There had been a time, in her teens, when she had actually contemplated running away to try to follow and find him. But that was then and this was now. A stable, adult woman did not go rushing after someone who clearly did not share her affection. He probably never had.

Still, she had to blink back unshed tears when she heard him gun the truck's engine and speed away, tires squealing.

Chapter Seven

Tony called himself every kind of fool. He never should have tried to convince Annette of his former loyalty, not when it meant turning her against her own mother. It would have to satisfy him that his conscience was clear. As for Mrs. Lakey, he'd back off and let the Lord handle the details.

Which, of course, was not easy. Turning problems over to God never was. Now that he realized his mistake, he could see why Annette had taken offense. The difference between him and her was that he knew the truth. Even if his mind had played a trick on him by insisting he'd left the planned farewell note when perhaps he had not, there was absolutely no doubt about the letters. Writing them had been a painstaking effort, one that he'd labored over for hours and hours.

Tony gritted his teeth. What he wanted to do

was go confront Annette's mother himself. What he would do, however, was cool off and bide his time—with the Lord's help.

A message waiting at the animal hospital when he returned to check was the answer to an unvoiced prayer. Tony quickly dialed the number.

"J.T. Sorry I missed your call. How's your mom?"

"Better. That's partly why I wanted to talk to you. I thought I'd stay longer than we'd planned if you have everything under control on your end. Do you?"

"Yeah, I'm fine. So far there's been nothing unusual. Just a litter of pups, the usual vaccinations and a couple of foundered horses." He snorted a chuckle. "Those guys are *big*."

"Most of 'em are. That's the whole idea," the senior veterinarian quipped. "They'd be hard to ride if your feet dragged on the ground."

"Speaking of riding, you do plan to be back before the rodeo starts, don't you? I mean, I can still stand in for you if I have to, but those bucking bulls and broncs are murder to work with."

"Now, see? I like them best. Show me a snappish little dog and I can hardly make myself touch it, let alone treat it. Together, you and I would add up being one pretty good vet." He paused for a few seconds. "If you ever decide you want to partner with me, let me know."

Tony huffed. "If you ever decide to move out of Jasper Gulch and go back to civilization, the same goes for you."

"Yeah, right. You know how unlikely that is. My roots are in Montana."

"Thankfully, mine aren't."

"You could do worse," his former mentor said. "Well, as long as you haven't run my practice into the ground or made my assistants quit yet, carry on."

"A week more, you said?"

"Give or take. You in a hurry to leave?"

Tony sighed. "No. Just wondering."

"You sound depressed. Have you had trouble living down your old reputation? I'd think not, considering the turnaround you made in life."

"There are a few holdouts," Tony admitted ruefully. "Nothing I can't handle."

The moment he made that claim, he knew it was untrue. He could face a raging mob without a qualm and still not know how to handle the only relationship that truly mattered to him. The one with Annette.

Bothered and curious in spite of herself, Annette was barely able to concentrate on her afternoon customers. While several older women snoozed under warm dryers, she finally gave in, grabbed her cell and hit speed dial.

Her grip on the phone tightened and she pressed it tightly to her ear while it rang.

"Hello?"

"Hi, Mom. It's me."

"Hi, honey! Good to hear from you. We're drying out after the storm faster than I'd expected. How about you?"

"Same here. Listen, I've been thinking. I wonder if you might help me remember something."

"If I can. What's this about?"

"Tony Valdez."

Dead silence ensued. Annette waited for her mother to say something, then gave up and continued with, "Remember him?"

"Unfortunately, yes. I was delighted when he left town."

"That's kind of why I'm calling. Do you recall him leaving me a note or sending me any letters?"

"Why would you ask such a thing?"

It was the strident tone of her mother's voice that triggered Annette's wariness. Could Tony have been telling the truth?

"Because I need to know," Annette insisted.

"That all happened a long time ago. I hardly even remember what he looked like. Just that he was a hoodlum. We were well rid of the likes of that boy."

"Maybe you were wrong about him. What if he grew up and became a model citizen?"

"The day I believe that will be the day they crown me Miss Jasper Gulch," her mother quipped. "Which reminds me, I still think you should enter."

"Eight or ten years ago maybe I'd have stood a chance. Twenty-six is far too old to compete with the Shoemaker girls."

"You should have taken my good advice when you were younger." Her mother sighed. "It's sad to see you miss wonderful opportunities that only come around once in a lifetime."

Once in a lifetime? It was impossible for Annette to stop thinking about the way she had idolized Tony and the faith she'd had that there was a good, honest person lurking beneath his tough facade; a person waiting for somebody like her to believe in him and bring out the best.

"You need to answer my question," Annette insisted, taking care to try to sound nonchalant. "Did Tony Valdez leave me a goodbye note?"

"I have no idea."

There was something off-putting about her mother's inflection; something that caused Annette to keep pressing. "Let me put it this way, Mom. Even if you didn't look to see what might have been inside envelopes addressed to me, were there any?"

"I suppose there could have been."

"Did you give them to me?"

"I must have. It's just been so long that you've forgotten."

"Un-uh. You may have chosen to put it out of your mind, but I never would have. I was hurting too badly in those days."

Annette was trembling so much she had to either sit down or fall down. While she searched for the strength to continue, the extended silence apparently triggered her mother to speak.

"You would have been hurt much worse if we'd let you get involved with that Tony or his no-good friends. I did you a favor and your father agreed. Those boys belonged in jail."

There it was. Tony was right. Annette's mother had blamed him for crimes he didn't commit and had kept his letters from reaching her. All this time she'd believed he didn't care when the opposite had been true.

Now, of course, everything was different. He was a college graduate with a professional career and she'd been left far behind. Through no fault of their own, they had drifted too far apart to ever belong together the way they once had.

A sense of enormous loss enveloped Annette. She ended her conversation with the click of a button and stuck the phone back in her pocket. When it began to ring almost immediately, she turned it off.

That was exactly how she felt, she realized. Disconnected and dead. The family she had always trusted had betrayed her. The person she had loved had been wronged, both in the past and by her recent rejection.

Could she ever hope to put that right? She strongly doubted it, yet she had to try. All the apologies in the world were not going to change the past, but perhaps she could at least soften Tony's anger and help him move on.

Without me, she admitted sadly. Well, so be it.

When he left Jasper Gulch in a few days or weeks, if she had anything to say about it, he'd go with his head held high and the stigma of his past erased. She could do no less.

Chapter Eight

Tony quickly realized he'd made a mistake by suggesting that Annette confront her mother. Any probing into their hazy, shared past would have to be her idea or she wouldn't be in the right frame of mind to accept the truth, when and if she heard it.

"Assuming Mrs. Lakey ever admits she did anything to keep me away from her daughter," Tony mumbled to himself as he turned onto Shaw Boulevard from Massey Street.

It had occurred to him to wonder if Annette's parents had been the ones to cast extra suspicion on him all those years ago, not that his buddies and their behavior had been totally innocent. A lot of his prior problems were nobody's fault but his own. He was just sorry it had taken him so long to realize he was headed down the wrong path. "Go to jail. Go directly to jail. Do not pass Go," as the card in the popular board game read.

Working for J.T. behind the scenes at the animal hospital had helped keep him off the streets as a teen, but it had not been enough to fully change the course of his wayward life. That had taken his parents' relocation and an intervention by a dedicated youth pastor.

Somewhere in the depths of his confusion and aching heart, Tony had found the path to Jesus and therefore to God. His reform had not been instantaneous, nor had it been accompanied by claps of thunder and bolts of lightning, but it had occurred just the same.

Was this another step in his rehabilitation? he wondered. Had the Lord engineered his return to Jasper Gulch? And if so, what was he supposed to accomplish while he was there?

The first thing that popped into his mind was an image of Annette. So pretty. So sweet. And yet also a strong, independent woman who ran her own business. In that respect, she was more stable, more settled, than he was. Establishing a veterinary practice was extremely expensive, which was one reason he'd accepted a part-time position as soon as he'd been licensed. It wasn't the kind of job he'd wanted to ultimately hold, but at least it had helped pay off his tuition loans. So had a second job as a lab tech. All in all, he'd had plenty to do; it had simply not been totally fulfilling.

Off to his left he could see the white-painted steeple of Mountainview Church of the Savior, the oldest house of worship in town and one of the most venerated buildings. Its presence called to him, as if offering the warm welcome he'd been denied by those who still viewed him as a juvenile delinquent.

Instead of continuing along Shaw Boulevard, Tony turned toward the old church. By the time he pulled into the gravel lot beside it and parked, he had decided to go in. Even if the pastor wasn't there he could sit silently in a pew and talk to God, try to make sense of what had been happening and the way his supposedly well-ordered life seemed to be in chaos.

Until he pushed on the side door, he hadn't considered that the building might be shut up tight.

Tony was turning to go when he heard a click behind him and a voice that said, "I'm here. Sorry. I guess Reverend Peters forgot to unlock the door." The man extended his hand. "Ethan Johnson. I'm going to be taking over Reverend Peters's position soon."

"Tony Valdez." They shook hands. "I hope you'll like it here."

"I'm sure I will. Are you a member of the congregation?" The pastor held open the door and stepped aside as an invitation to enter.

Hesitating, Tony smiled at him. "No, just visiting. I don't even know why I'm standing here except that I was driving by and had a crazy urge to stop."

"Oh?"

Tony nodded. "Yeah. I'm beginning to get the idea that God may have sent me back to Montana to make amends for my past mistakes."

"Would you like to come in and talk about it? I have an hour or so free before the current pastor is treating me to an orientation tour."

Tony checked his watch. "Thanks, but I'll have to take a rain check. I'm on my way out to the Shaw ranch to check a couple of heifers."

"Oh, are you the new veterinarian?" Ethan beamed at him. "I've heard about you." Once again he extended a hand of greeting and acceptance.

"And you still want to shake my hand?" Tony returned his grin. "That's very Christian of you."

Chuckling, Ethan clasped Tony's right hand with both of his and said, "My pleasure."

The next few days with Stormy and her pups were fairly uneventful. The noises the little ones made as they blindly explored their tiny world were adorable and surprisingly soothing, so much so that when they were all asleep Annette missed their soft squeaks and murmurs.

The mama dog had gotten into the habit of feeding her babies, then cuddling with them and napping for a while before hopping out and joining Annette. Nearly every time she turned around, there was Stormy, either curled up nearby or wagging her bushy tail and looking at her with eager expectation.

"Well, at least it's warmed up outside," Annette told the dog. "Would you like to go for a walk, girl?"

Stormy's tail rapidly traced figure eights in the air.

"I'll take that as a yes." Annette laughed at herself. "Here I stand, having a conversation with a dog and believing we actually understand each other." She rolled her eyes. "All I wanted was to do a good deed. Who would have thought it would come to this?"

"I would have," a deep, masculine voice behind her said.

Annette jumped as if receiving an electric shock. "Oh! Tony! I didn't hear you come in."

"Sorry if I scared you."

It was a far more complicated feeling than that, she admitted silently. Yes, her heart was pounding and she was having trouble getting enough oxygen, but that had little to do with being startled. If someone like old Rusty had come in without her noticing, the shock would *not* have lingered and made her insides quiver.

She didn't have to force a smile. It blossomed unbidden. If she could have found adequate words she would have asked him if he could ever forgive her for doubting him. The sooner she revealed her full conversation with her mother, the better, yet she hardly knew where to begin.

"How are your furry roommates?" he asked.

"Fine, I think." Annette laid her hand lightly on Stormy's head and ruffled her silky ears. "When will the pups open their eyes and start to explore?"

"Another week or so should do it." Tony came toward her. "Mind if I take a look?"

Backing up to give herself breathing room, she reached for the frayed red ribbon.

"Hold on. I brought you something," Tony said. He produced a roll of leather from his jacket pocket. "A collar and leash. I'll get her vaccinations up to date before I leave town and give you the tag to attach."

Watching him adjust the collar around the dog's neck, Annette fought back tears. His hands were strong yet his touch was gentle. It didn't matter what had happened in his past; he had become a good, good man, one she was proud to know.

"I…"

"No, me first," Tony said. "I need to apologize for saying what I did about your mother."

"No, no. You were right," Annette insisted.

His expression was solemn and sad, even though a slight smile lifted one corner of his mouth. "It doesn't matter. I've given it a lot of thought, and I realize there's no reason to dig up old grudges."

Meaning, he had no intention of discussing it further or giving her a chance to make amends. Well, she wasn't going to give up on him. On *them.*

"I think we should talk it out," Annette said flatly.

"There's nothing to talk about."

Now what? Should she continue to press him or back off for the present? A lot depended on how soon he'd be leaving town. The one thing she was not going to do was let him go away again without telling him that she believed in him.

"I think there is. I got my mother to admit she withheld your letters. I know you were telling me the truth."

"Good."

"That's it? That's all you have to say?"

Tony slowly shook his head. His gaze met hers and held. "What else is there?" His expression hardened before he went on. "If you had believed me before you found out what she'd done, there might be more to talk about. You made your choice, Annette."

Rebuttal would have felt good if she could have come up with a reasonable excuse for her prior behavior. Unfortunately, she knew he was right. If she'd truly accepted him, she would have trusted and defended him, just as she had in her teens. She had doubted instead. And now she would pay the consequences.

"All right. Make yourself at home with the pups while I take Stormy for a walk," she said, following her statement with a sigh.

Tony paused by the puppies while Annette bent to clip the leash to the collar before leading her canine companion out into the sunshine. Away from Tony. And away from a problem she had no idea how to remedy.

A ridiculous thought had her envisioning herself, prostrate with grief at Tony's feet, grabbing his ankles, wailing like a child having a tantrum, sobbing out her repentance and vowing everlasting love.

She rolled her eyes. That was *so* not going to happen.

Chapter Nine

Disgusted with himself for letting his temper get the better of him, Tony left the pups and went to wash up. The slam of a door echoed a few moments later.

Tony was drying his hands as he emerged from the bathroom. "Oh, hi, Rusty. Annette'll be right back. She's walking the dog."

"And what're you up to?"

"Me? I came to check the pups. How about you?"

"Never you mind," the old man said gruffly. "What I want to know is why you're hangin' around so much and makin' yourself at home here." His bushy eyebrows knit. "It ain't good for Miss Annette to have a man goin' in and out the way you've been."

"It doesn't seem to bother you to do it."

"When you get to be as old as I am, folks cut you some slack. Besides, I'm old enough to know better," Rusty countered. "You, on the other hand…"

"Will not be in Jasper Gulch one minute longer than necessary," Tony assured him.

"That so?"

"Yes. That's so."

Rusty shrugged his bony shoulders beneath a worn denim jacket. "You *sure* about that?"

Tony could feel his stare cutting to the bone. Was he sure? Of course he was. Yet…

"Uh-huh. That's what I thought," Rusty said when Tony failed to continue. "Just don't you go breakin' the lady's heart again, you hear? Or you'll have to answer to me."

"I'd never do anything like that on purpose," Tony insisted. "I didn't the first time, either."

"Then how come she says you did?"

Tony decided it wouldn't hurt to speak his mind. "She doesn't. Not anymore. I wrote to her after my family moved. She didn't get my letters."

"Her mama." It wasn't a question. "Figures." Rusty removed his beat-up Stetson and ran his gnarled fingers through his hair. "Miz Lakey always was one to climb up on her high horse a lot, if you get my drift. How'd Annette find out?"

Shrugging, Tony hoped he looked a lot more nonchalant than he was feeling. "She asked her."

"Good. Then why the long face, son?"

"It's complicated."

Rusty gave him a lopsided smile and arched one eyebrow. "You sure about that? Seems to me she wouldn't have asked in the first place if she didn't sort of believe your story."

"*Sort of* doesn't cut it."

"Suit yourself. Looks like it would do you both a load of good if you set aside the past and just got on with enjoyin' the future." He chortled. "You was the one askin' for a fresh start. Suppose you give her one, too?"

The old man's country wisdom left him speechless.

It also created the question of how Tony could possibly make amends and whether or not Annette would be able to forgive him for doing the same thing he had accused her of.

There was an additional element to that puzzle, too. How to heal the breach between them without giving the impression that he was only trying to take up where they'd left off ten years before.

One thing was clear. It was time for a heart-to-heart, no-holds-barred conversation, and since he'd refused to participate when she had suggested the very same solution, it was going to be up to him to make it happen.

Annette had almost hoped Tony would be gone by the time she returned from walking Stormy. Instead, it looked as if he'd been waiting for her. Not only that, there was a seriousness to his demeanor that took her by surprise.

Her first reaction was worry. "Are the puppies all right?"

"They're fine. Fat and sassy."

"Then why…?"

"I've been waiting for you."

"Why?"

When he answered "Because I've been wrong," she stared.

"About what?"

"About judging you. It wasn't fair of me to want you to blindly trust me when I was assuming the worst about you, too."

She arched an eyebrow. "The worst? How?"

"I didn't give you the benefit of the doubt concerning your mother's past actions. I know you couldn't help doubting me when you naturally trusted your parents to be straight with you." He cleared his throat. "I mean, it's normal for kids to look up to their folks and believe them, even if they're twisting the truth."

Annette heaved a noisy sigh and began to shake her head. "Exactly. I'm still having trouble grasping the entire story. She said she and Dad were just trying to protect me."

"From me, obviously."

"Yes. And you really can't blame them when

you look at the situation as an adult. You and I had little in common and were far too young to know what lasting love was."

The slight smile that twitched at the corners of Tony's mouth made him so attractive she wanted to throw her arms around his neck and give him a conciliatory kiss. Instead, she let herself smile back at him while adding, "We were just caught up in the moment, the confusion of teenage angst and the idea of a fairy-tale romance. At least I know I was."

"Right," Tony agreed. "We were dumb kids."

"Not dumb, simply naive. Who knows how far wrong we might have gone if circumstances hadn't split us up. It was just hard to let go of the fantasy that we were a couple. At least it was for me."

"What about now? Have you thought about that?"

Another sigh punctuated her reply as she nodded. "Yes, actually I have. Logically, we're even less likely to belong together than we did years ago." She spread her arms wide. "Look at us. What do we have in common now?"

He eyed the puppies and waggled his eyebrows. "Fur babies?"

"Right." She grinned. "And their mama. What am I going to do with them? I finally did post flyers and have had zero response. Not even a query."

"If you have trouble finding new homes I suppose I could take one of them with me once they're weaned in a few more weeks. Stormy is the logical one to stay with you since she's house-broken."

Annette opened her mouth to protest about keeping a pet the way she usually did, then snapped it closed. He was right. She already loved the dogs' companionship and knew her life would feel even more empty if she gave them all away. Added to that, of course, was the constant attention the litter had brought from her favorite veterinarian. *That* was what she was going to miss the most.

The notion of expressing such a telling truth came and went in a flash. It was clear from Tony's standoffish attitude and the way he'd changed the subject that he had no intention of staying in Jasper Gulch, not even for her sake. The only way to preserve what little pride she had left was to keep her most tender sentiments to herself.

But oh, my, she was going to miss him.

The next Sunday morning dawned bright and fair. It was Tony's third in Jasper Gulch, if he counted the day of his arrival, and he'd made up his mind to go to church.

Biblically, he was "putting out the fleece," meaning he was asking God for confirmation about his change of heart the same way Gideon had in the Old Testament book of Judges. He'd already had an in-depth conversation with J.T. about the possibility of joining his practice and knew where he stood in that regard. The opportunity was real. All that was left was to decide what to do about it.

There was no assurance that sticking around would make Annette care for him again, but he wanted to give their relationship a fair chance. If these citizens of Jasper Gulch acted as if they accepted him into their congregation, he'd take that as a favorable sign and proceed with his new plans. If they did not, he'd have to rethink everything. The last thing he wanted to do was cause damage, however innocently, to Annette's business and reputation.

Elderly Reverend Peters greeted him as if they were old friends, making Tony wonder if the old man was more confused than friendly. However, when stranger after stranger smiled and shook his hand, Tony began to grin. So far so good.

When he spotted Annette at a distance, his heart began to race and he suddenly realized he had his answer. Overall tolerance was not necessary as long as one particular woman accepted him. The choice was made.

Nearby conversation lessened and her friends changed their focus, causing Annette to look behind her.

"Tony!"

He reached for her hand, thrilled when she didn't pull away. "I was hoping I'd find you here."

"I wasn't lost. You know where I live and work."

"I know. That didn't come out right. Nothing does when I'm trying to talk to you."

Annette smiled at him. "I know what you mean."

"We should start over," he said.

She shook her head. "Uh-uh. No way. You're about to leave again and I'm still struggling with the last time you dropped out of my life."

"Suppose I told you I've given it some serious thought and changed my mind? Would that please you?"

"What do you mean?"

"I've been talking to J.T. He's always preferred doctoring large animals and I like dogs and cats, so we came up with a solution. He's offered me a partnership if I want it."

"Here? In Jasper Gulch? But you hate it here."

"It's actually not that bad. I think I got so used to putting the place down, I didn't even consider the fact that my feelings about living here had changed."

Her jaw dropped. Tony lifted it with one finger under her chin and began to grin. "Does this mean you're glad?"

All she could do was nod rapidly as a few happy

tears slipped down her cheeks and his thumb whisked them away.

She sniffled. "You're—you're staying? In spite of all the wild-and-woolly farm animals coming to town for the rodeo soon?"

"Yes. J.T. should be back by July, but even if he isn't, I'll manage." He grinned. "We'll manage. If it's okay with you, I'd like to see if you and I can make something good out of our troubled past."

"I like the way your mind works, mister." She gave a soft chuckle and saw his puzzled expression, so she hurried to explain. "I guess this means I can stop trying to decide how much to ask for the Cutting Edge."

"What?"

"I was seriously thinking of selling out and following you wherever you ended up."

"You were going to leave Jasper Gulch? For me?"

Annette nodded. "If that was my only option. I let you go away once, when I was too young to do anything about it. I decided I shouldn't give up on you—on us—this time."

She leaned into his shoulder as he slipped an arm around her and pulled her closer.

"We have a lot of lost time to make up for," Tony said, whispering just for her.

"And the kids to think of. Stormy and the gang would miss you too much if you left us."

"Right. I thought I'd make her my mascot," Tony said. "You know that empty storefront next to your shop? J.T.'s looking into renting it as a satellite office for the small-animal part of the practice. You and I will be neighbors. We can share custody of Stormy until we've had more chance to get reacquainted and plan for the future."

"I don't think that's going to take very long."

"Whenever you're ready, honey. There's no rush. I'm not going anywhere. I promise you won't have to worry about losing me again. Not ever."

Gazing up at him, Annette had no doubt. God had answered her prayers and brought her first love back to her. She was never going to stop giving thanks for such a special blessing, such an extraordinary man.

"Good!" She broke into a face-splitting grin. "And if my mother or anybody else gives me grief about spending the rest of my life with you, I'll tell her we have to stay together for the sake of our furry friends."

Tony laughed and pulled her closer for a brief hug. "Works for me."

* * * * *

If you enjoyed this prequel novella to the
BIG SKY CENTENNIAL *miniseries,*
be sure to read all six books in this miniseries
from Love Inspired:

Book #1: HER MONTANA COWBOY
by Valerie Hansen
When rodeo cowboy Ryan Travers comes to
town, mayor's daughter Julie Shaw can't keep
her eyes off him. Amid Jasper Gulch's centen-
nial celebrations, they just may find true love!

Book #2: HIS MONTANA SWEETHEART
by Ruth Logan Herne
Olivia Franklin never imagined coming home
would mean running into first love Jack
McGuire. Can working together on the town's
centennial celebration give these former sweet-
hearts a second chance at forever?

Book #3: HER MONTANA TWINS
by Carolyne Aarsen
Handsome firefighter Brody Harcourt has
always had a soft spot for Hannah Douglas.
When they're thrown together in the midst of the
town's centennial celebrations, can Brody con-
vince the widowed mom of twins to give love
another try?

Book #4: HIS MONTANA BRIDE
by Brenda Minton
*Cord Shaw's had enough of romance. So when
he and pretty Katie Archer are suddenly in
charge of a fifty-couple wedding in honor of the
town's centennial celebration, he's surprised
when he's one of the grooms saying I do.*

Book #5: HIS MONTANA HOMECOMING
by Jenna Mindel
*Millionaire Dale Massey has come to Jasper
Gulch's centennial celebration to honor his
family—nothing more. But he quickly sees the
joys of small-town life—and a potential future
with charming Faith Shaw.*

Book #6: HER MONTANA CHRISTMAS
by Arlene James
*When town historian Robin Frazier agrees to
help Pastor Ethan Johnson decorate the church
for a centennial Christmas celebration, she
never expected to fall for him. Will revealing her
secret ruin everything?*

Love Inspired

YOU HAVE JUST READ A LOVE INSPIRED® BOOK.

If you enjoyed this heartwarming story of faith, forgiveness and hope, be sure to look for all six Love Inspired® books every month.

Turn the page for savings on your next purchase!

HALOLISMP14

Love Inspired

Her Montana Twins
by
Carolyne Aarsen

Raising twins on her own hasn't been easy for widowed mom
Hannah Douglas. But she's determined to see her family—and the
picnic basket auction she's organizing for the town's centennial
celebration—succeed. Still, there are times she wishes for someone
to lean on. To her surprise, Brody Harcourt's strong shoulders are
at the ready. Seems like Jasper Gulch's favorite firefighter and
rancher is always there when she needs him. But Hannah's not
sure she's willing to take another chance on love, especially with
someone whose job puts him in harm's way. Is the risk of loving
Brody worth the reward to make her family complete?

BIG SKY
CENTENNIAL

A small town rich in history…and love.

*Available September 2014
wherever Love Inspired books and ebooks are sold.*

LI87907

Love Inspired

Use this coupon to
SAVE $1.00
on the purchase of
ANY
Love Inspired® book!

Available wherever books are sold.

SAVE $1.00 ON THE PURCHASE OF **ANY** LOVE INSPIRED® BOOK.

Coupon expires December 31, 2014. Valid only at participating Walmart stores. Limit one coupon per customer. Coupons are void where prohibited, taxed or otherwise restricted by law.

CANADIAN RETAILERS: Harlequin Enterprises Limited will pay the face value of this coupon plus 10.25¢ if submitted by customer for this product only. Any other use constitutes fraud. Coupon is nonassignable. Void if taxed, prohibited or restricted by law. Consumer must pay any government taxes. Void if copied. Millennium1 Promotional Services ("M1P") customers submit coupons and proof of sales to Harlequin Enterprises Limited, P.O. Box 3000, Saint John, NB E2L 4L3, Canada. Non-M1P retailer—for reimbursement submit coupons and proof of sales directly to Harlequin Enterprises Limited, Retail Marketing Department, 225 Duncan Mill Rd., Don Mills, ON M3B 3K9, Canada.

U.S. RETAILERS: Harlequin Enterprises Limited will pay the face value of this coupon plus 8¢ if submitted by customer for this product only. Any other use constitutes fraud. Coupon is nonassignable. Void if taxed, prohibited or restricted by law. Consumer must pay any government taxes. Void if copied. For reimbursement submit coupons and proof of sales directly to Harlequin Enterprises Limited, P.O. Box 880478, El Paso, TX 88588-0478, U.S.A. Cash value 1/100 cents.

52611807

5 65373 00076 2   (8100)0 11961

Love Inspired®
SUSPENSE
RIVETING INSPIRATIONAL ROMANCE

AROUND-THE-CLOCK PROTECTOR

Despite the threats against her life, Danielle Barclay thinks having a bodyguard is unnecessary. Or at least that's what she tells herself before meeting Jake Rabb. A former Delta Force solider, Jake is used to rope-lining from helicopters into enemy territory—not following around a senator's daughter. The lovely deputy district attorney is as strong-willed as she is brave, especially when the escalating danger assures Jake that her stalker means business. As the attacks become personal, Danielle finally puts her trust—and her feelings—on the line with her defender. But how will Jake protect her if the stalker is closer than they think?

KEEPING WATCH
by
JANE M. CHOATE

*Available October 2014 wherever
Love Inspired books and ebooks are sold.*

LIS44629

SUSPENSE

RIVETING INSPIRATIONAL ROMANCE

Use this coupon to

SAVE $1.00

on the purchase of

ANY

Love Inspired®
Suspense book!

Available wherever books are sold.

SAVE $1.00 ON THE PURCHASE OF **ANY** LOVE INSPIRED® SUSPENSE BOOK.

Coupon expires December 31, 2014. Valid only at participating Walmart stores. Limit one coupon per customer. Coupons are void where prohibited, taxed or otherwise restricted by law.

52611810

5 65373 00076 2   **(8100)0 11962**

CANADIAN RETAILERS: Harlequin Enterprises Limited will pay the face value of this coupon plus 10.25¢ if submitted by customer for this product only. Any other use constitutes fraud. Coupon is nonassignable. Void if taxed, prohibited or restricted by law. Consumer must pay any government taxes. Void if copied. Millennium1 Promotional Services ("M1P") customers submit coupons and proof of sales to Harlequin Enterprises Limited, P.O. Box 3000, Saint John, NB E2L 4L3, Canada. Non-M1P retailer—for reimbursement submit coupons and proof of sales directly to Harlequin Enterprises Limited, Retail Marketing Department, 225 Duncan Mill Rd., Don Mills, ON M3B 3K9, Canada.

U.S. RETAILERS:
Harlequin Enterprises Limited will pay the face value of this coupon plus 8¢ if submitted by customer for this product only. Any other use constitutes fraud. Coupon is nonassignable. Void if taxed, prohibited or restricted by law. Consumer must pay any government taxes. Void if copied. For reimbursement submit coupons and proof of sales directly to Harlequin Enterprises Limited, P.O. Box 880478, El Paso, TX 88588-0478, U.S.A. Cash value 1/100 cents.

LISCOUP0914

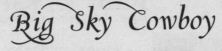

Big Sky Cowboy

by LINDA FORD

JUST THE COWBOY SHE NEEDED?

The last thing Cora Bell wants is a distracting cowboy showing up on her family's farm seeking temporary shelter. Especially one she is sure has something to hide. But she'll accept Wyatt Williams's help rebuilding her family's barn—and try not to fall once again for a man whose plans don't include staying around.

Since leaving his troubled past behind, Wyatt avoids personal entanglements. He just wants to make a new start with his younger brother. But there's something about Cora that he's instinctively drawn to. Dare this solitary cowboy risk revealing his secrets for a chance at redemption and a bright new future with Cora by his side?

Montana
Marriages

Three sisters discover a legacy
of love beneath the Western sky

*Available October 2014 wherever
Love Inspired books and ebooks are sold.*

LIH28282

Love Inspired HISTORICAL

Use this coupon to

SAVE $1.00

on the purchase of
ANY
Love Inspired®
Historical book!

Available wherever books are sold.

SAVE $1.00 ON THE PURCHASE OF **ANY** LOVE INSPIRED® HISTORICAL BOOK.

Coupon expires December 31, 2014. Valid only at participating Walmart stores. Limit one coupon per customer. Coupons are void where prohibited, taxed or otherwise restricted by law.

52611823

5 65373 00076 2   (8100)0 11963

LIHCOUP0914

BIG SKY CENTENNIAL

A small town rich in history…and love.

As the tiny all-American town prepares to celebrate its one hundredth anniversary, folks aren't expecting a six-month whirlwind of romantic surprises.

Her Montana Cowboy by Valerie Hansen
July 2014

His Montana Sweetheart by Ruth Logan Herne
August 2014

Her Montana Twins by Carolyne Aarsen
September 2014

His Montana Bride by Brenda Minton
October 2014

His Montana Homecoming by Jenna Mindel
November 2014

Her Montana Christmas by Arlene James
December 2014

*Available wherever books
and ebooks are sold.*

Find us on Facebook at
www.Facebook.com/LoveInspiredBooks